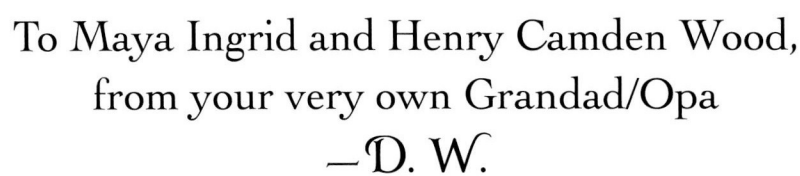

To Maya Ingrid and Henry Camden Wood,
from your very own Grandad/Opa
—D. W.

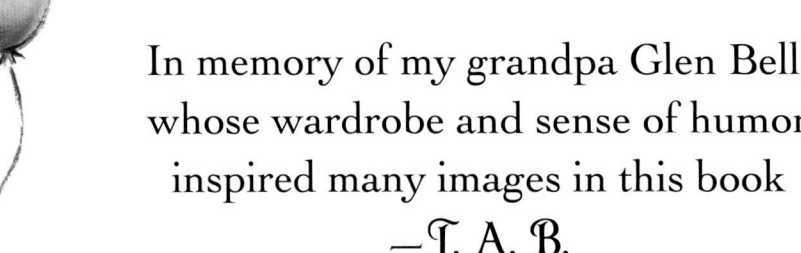

In memory of my grandpa Glen Bell,
whose wardrobe and sense of humor
inspired many images in this book
—J. A. B.

SIMON & SCHUSTER BOOKS FOR YOUNG READERS
An imprint of Simon & Schuster Children's Publishing Division
1230 Avenue of the Americas, New York, New York 10020
Text copyright © 2014 by Douglas Wood
Illustrations copyright © 2014 by Jennifer A. Bell
SIMON & SCHUSTER BOOKS FOR YOUNG READERS is a trademark of Simon & Schuster, Inc.
For information about special discounts for bulk purchases, please contact Simon & Schuster Special Sales
at 1-866-506-1949 or business@simonandschuster.com.
The Simon & Schuster Speakers Bureau can bring authors to your live event. For more information or to book an event,
contact the Simon & Schuster Speakers Bureau
at 1-866-248-3049 or visit our website at www.simonspeakers.com.
Book design by Chloë Foglia
The text for this book is set in Cochin.
The illustrations for this book are rendered in pencil and then finished digitally.
Manufactured in China
0514 SCP
10 9 8 7 6 5 4 3 2 1
Library of Congress Cataloging-in-Publication Data
Wood, Douglas, 1951–
When a grandpa says "I love you" / Douglas Wood ; illustrated by Jennifer A. Bell.
pages cm
Summary: Explores some of the many and varied ways a grandfather can express his love, even without saying the words,
such as by sharing his coin collection, holding hands when crossing the street, and attending tea parties.
ISBN 978-0-689-81512-6 (hardcover)
ISBN 978-1-4424-9847-1 (eBook)
[1. Grandfathers—Fiction. 2. Love—Fiction.] I. Bell, Jennifer (Jennifer A.), 1977– illustrator. II. Title.
PZ7.W84738Wji 2014
[E]—dc23
2012047773

When a grandpa says "I love you,"
he doesn't always say it
in the regular way.
That would be just a little bit too . . . regular.

Instead, he might just say something like,
"How would you like crêpes suzette for breakfast?"

Even if neither one of you is quite sure what they are.

Sometimes a grandpa says "I love you" by mussing up your hair. *Just* after you've combed it.

He might say it by teaching you how to wink.
Even though it never quite works.

Or by showing you
how to tie your tennis shoes.
Again.

A grandpa can say "I love you" by taking you for a walk,
and by holding your hand when you cross the street.
Just to make sure *he's* safe.

He can say it by watching you
do somersaults.

And cartwheels. (Almost.)

And by giving you
a standing ovation.

He might say "I love you" by buying you
a double-scoop ice-cream cone
on a hot summer day.

And then by helping you eat it
if it melts too fast.

A grandpa can say "I love you"
by letting you help him weed the garden.
And pick the tomatoes.
And water the roses.

He might say it by teaching you
how to throw a super-duper,
screaming yellow zonker sinker ball.

And then by striking out
when you throw it!

Sometimes a grandpa says "I love you"
by showing you his coin collection.
And then by giving you the shiniest one.

A grandpa can say "I love you" by coming
to your very own tea party.
And pretending that he *loves* tea.

He could show you how to play old-fashioned games, like checkers or Parcheesi or cribbage. . . .

Or he might try to learn a new game that you can teach him!
(Even on the computer.)

A grandpa can say "I love you" by letting you carry "top secret" messages across enemy lines. To Grandma.

He can say it by telling you
the kind of stories that only a grandpa can tell.
The kind that make the whole world seem . . . special.

And make you feel that
you are the most special person in it.

But most of all, a grandpa says
"I love you" just by being . . .

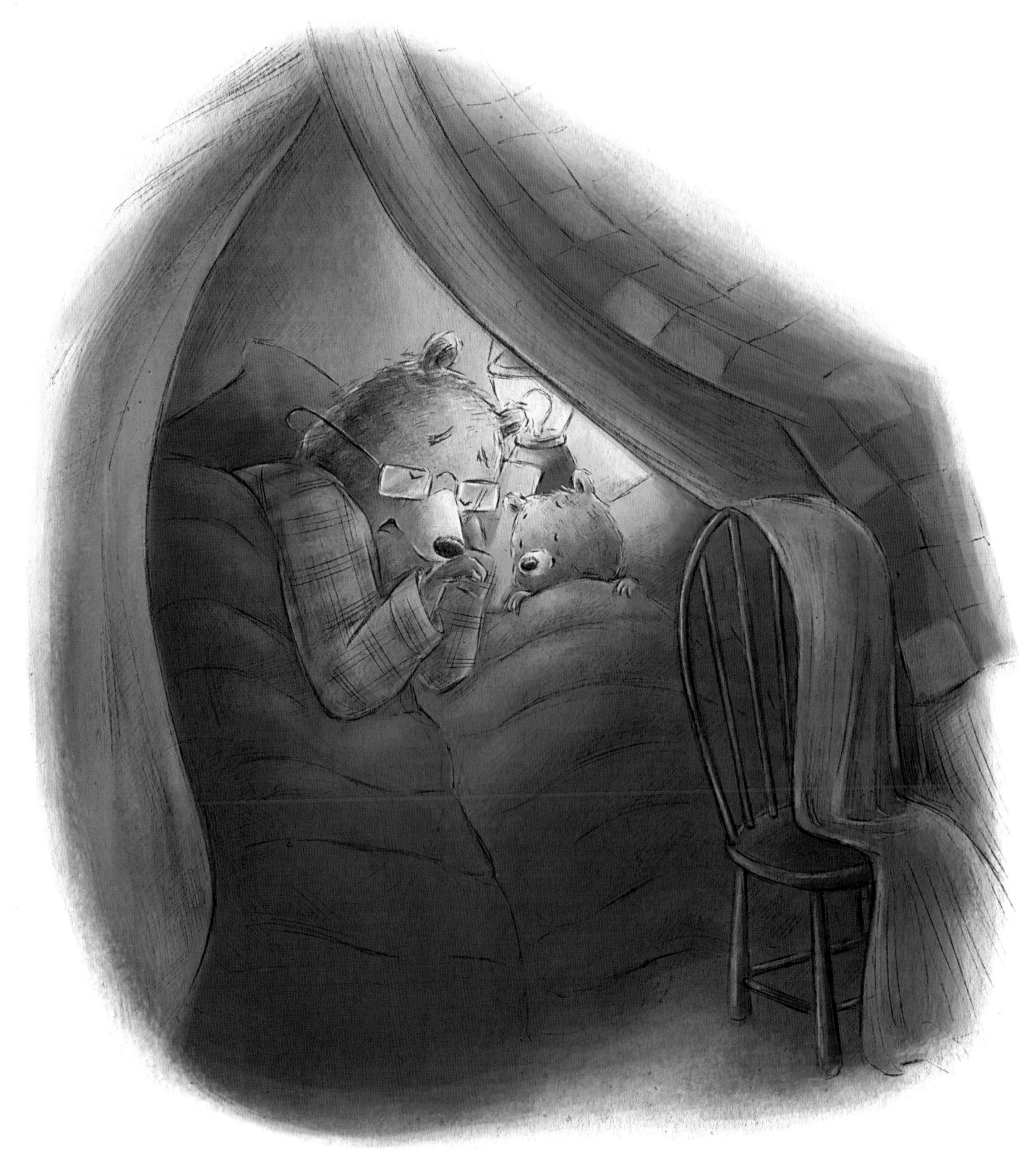

your grandpa!